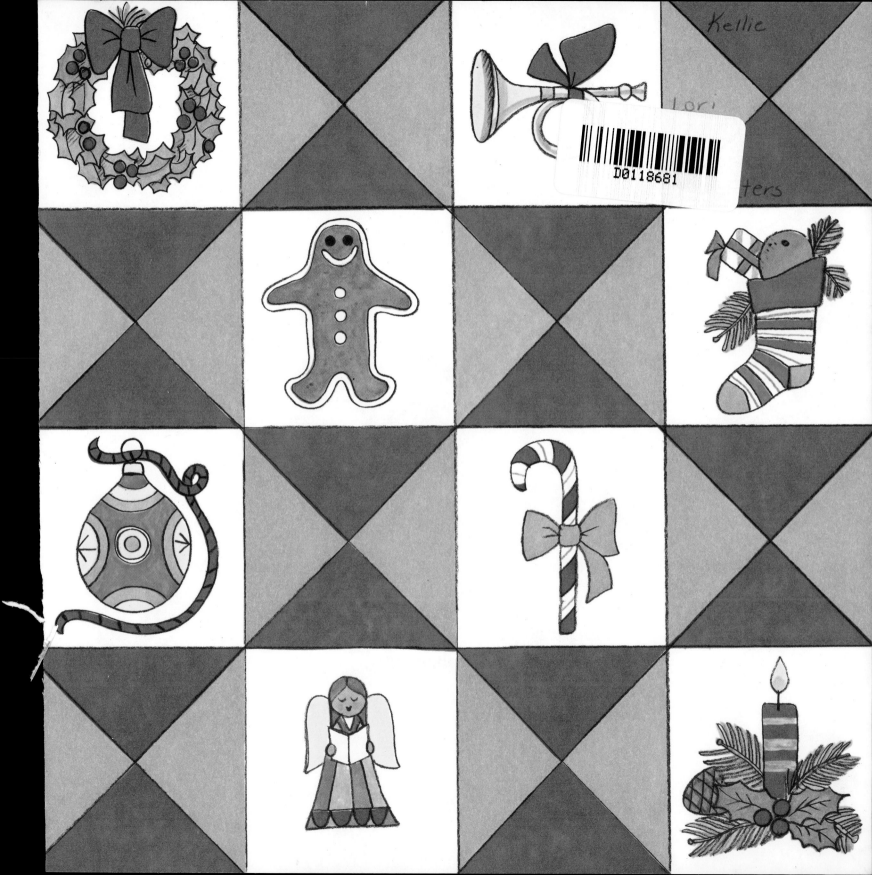

Little Bear says:
"*When you see a fragrance label,*
scratch it with your fingernail.
You will smell Christmas, too."

The Sweet Smell of Christmas

by Patricia Scarry

pictures by J. P. Miller

Copyright © 1970 by Western Publishing Company, Inc. Printed in the U.S.A.
GOLDEN®, A GOLDEN SCRATCH AND SNIFF BOOK, and GOLDEN PRESS® are trademarks of Western Publishing Company, Inc.
Library of Congress Catalog Card Number: 78-119327

The "Microfragrance"™ labels were supplied by 3M Company.

 GOLDEN PRESS • NEW YORK
Western Publishing Company, Inc.
Racine, Wisconsin

One morning, Little Bear sat up in bed and sniffed and sniffed with his nose. "Something wonderful is going to happen," he said. "My nose tells me so."

Little Bear ran downstairs to the kitchen.
"Mommy, what do I smell?" he asked.
"Christmas is coming. I think that's
what you smell," said Mother Bear.
"When will Christmas be here, mommy?"

"Christmas will be here tomorrow. I'm
baking this apple pie for Christmas."
Little Bear sniffed at the pie. It smelled
delicious! "Yes, I can smell Christmas.
It's coming soon," he said.

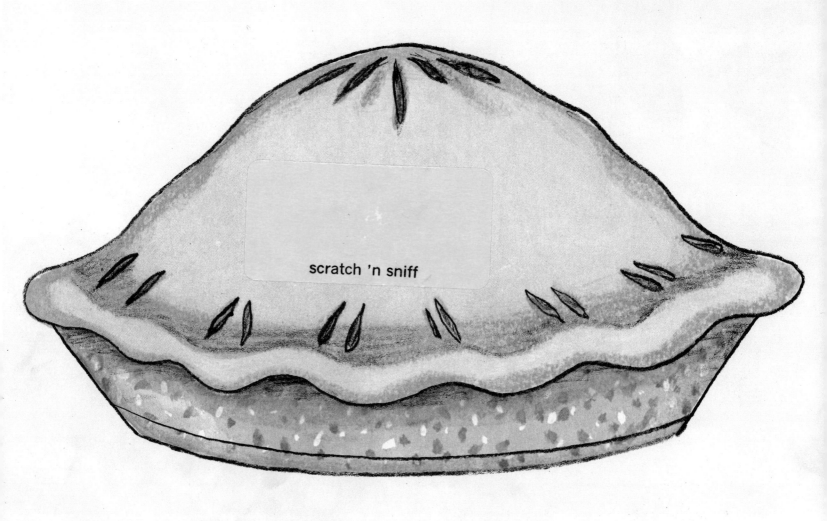

scratch 'n sniff

Here is Bear's apple pie.
Can you smell Christmas, too?

After breakfast, Father Bear pulled
Little Bear on his sled. "Are we going
to find Christmas, daddy?"
asked Bear.
"No, we are going to find
a nice little pine tree to take
home for our Christmas tree,"
said father.

They searched in the woods until they found a
bushy little pine tree. Father chopped it down with
his axe and put it on the sled.

Little Bear helped pull the tree home over the snow. It was a nice fresh tree, and it smelled so piney. Little Bear poked his nose into the branches and sniffed a deep sniff. "Now I can smell Christmas," he said. "It's not far away."

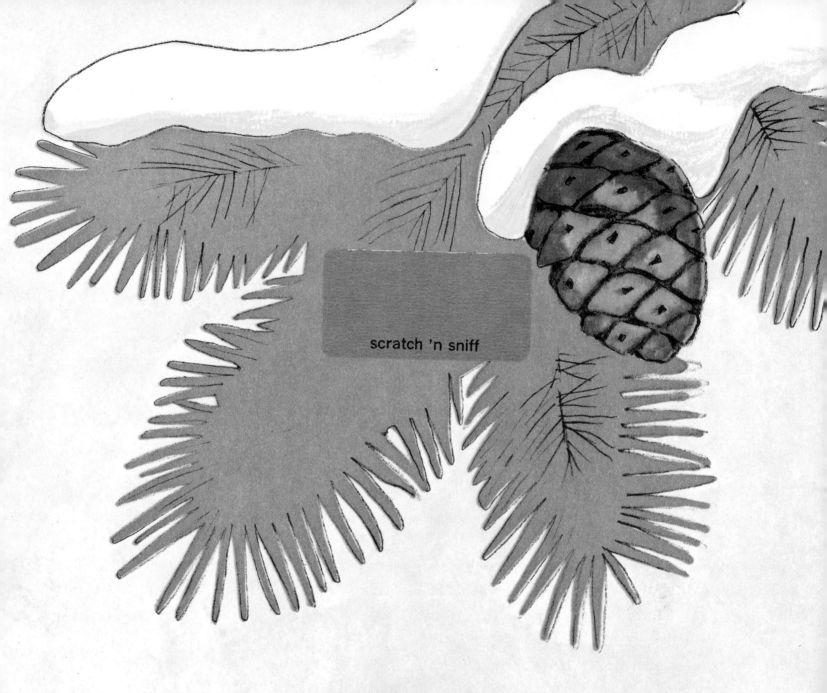

You smell the pine tree, too.
Doesn't it smell nice?

Then the Bear family trimmed their tree. It was fun! They hung lovely glass balls and silvery tinsel on the branches. On the very top, father put a beautiful star.

"Something is missing," said mother. "What can it be?"

She hurried to the kitchen. When she came back, she was carrying a big jar. "Candy canes," she said. "We forgot to put candy canes on our tree."

Bear held a candy cane in his paw and sniffed. "Mmmm, I can smell Christmas. It's coming very soon!" he said.

scratch 'n sniff

Here is a candy cane
for you to sniff.

Can you smell
Christmas coming?

Little Bear hung the candy canes on the branches. At last, the tree was finished. And, oh my, it was so beautiful! Little Bear jumped up and down and clapped his paws.

Mother Bear was working in the kitchen.
"What are you making, mommy?"
asked Bear.
"Gingerbread boys," said mother.
"You may help me."
Bear liked doing that. He cut out the

gingerbread boys with a little tin cutter.
Then he made their funny faces.
And when he smelled them cooking,
Bear said, "Mmmm, I can smell
Christmas. It's almost here!"

scratch 'n sniff

This is your gingerbread boy.
Does it smell like Christmas, too?

While Bear was hanging a gingerbread boy on the tree, he heard singing at the window. There, in the snow, were some carolers. How lovely it was to hear Christmas music in the frosty night.

Mother Bear invited the carolers indoors for some steaming hot chocolate. Bear had some, too. He put his nose down close to his cup. The hot chocolate smelled sweet and chocolatey. "Oh, now I can smell Christmas," Bear said. "It's going to happen right away!"

scratch 'n sniff

Now you smell the hot chocolate.
Mmmm. It smells so good.

Bear was right. It was almost Christmas. The Bear family hung their stockings by the fireplace. Then Little Bear hurried to bed. He listened for Santa's reindeer landing on the roof. He listened and listened. Then he fell asleep.

"Ho! Ho! Ho!" laughed merry Santa Claus, as he slid down the chimney. "My, what a pretty tree," he said, nibbling a gingerbread boy, "and what a good little bear lives here. I will leave him lots of toys." He dug in his toysack and put everything a bear could dream of under the tree.

At last, it was morning. Little Bear woke up.
He sniffed. He said, "It's Christmas day at last!"
Then he ran downstairs to find his stocking. There
was a big juicy orange on top, and down inside,
Bear found a little red train, a storybook,
a tiny ball, and candies and puzzles.
Bear sniffed at his orange.
"Now I know it's Christmas!" he said.
And he ate that orange up.

scratch 'n sniff

Here is a
Christmas orange
for you.

Can you smell Christmas now?

Mother and Father Bear hurried downstairs to open their presents, too. There was a nice tie for father, and warm mittens. Mother found a necklace and lots of pretty things.

And under the tree for Little Bear were a big red scooter, a drum, a little toy horse, a bugle and a big striped ball. Best of all, there was a soft furry teddy bear, a Christmas friend for Bear. All the Bears agreed it was the happiest Christmas ever!